SCARY BONES
THE SKELETON

The Fourth Adventure

Scary Bones meets the
Wacky Witches of Wareham

By

Ron Dawson

Illustrated by Sue Burleigh

First Published in 2011 by Mulberry Tree Books

Printed and bound in the UK by Imprintdigital, Exeter EX5 5HY.

This is a photograph of Corfe Castle near Wareham where most of this adventure happens.

● ●

MTBooks

Mulberry Tree Books, Mulberry House, Winterborne Stickland, Dorset DT11 0NT
www.mulberrytreebooks.co.uk

ISBN 978-0-9561732-5-

The Fourth Adventure:
<u>Scary Bones Meets the</u>
<u>Wacky Witches of Wareham</u>

Chapter 1

Sasha and Ben were staying with their Grandma for a few days while their parents were attending to some important nonsense or other, the sort that grownups always seem to be bothering about. The children didn't mind because they liked to stay with their Grandma in her house which is right in the middle of the little town of Wareham.

From their bedroom window at the front of her house they could see a bridge over a river. There were always lots of little boats on the river sailing backwards and forwards to Poole Harbour and Brownsea Island without any other purpose than to sail there and back, and then to sail back and there again. From another of their bedroom windows they could see the town church and the graveyard right behind it. The graveyard was so big that it seemed to go on for ever and ever, and perhaps even further than that. Then, from the last window in their bedroom, they could see the crossroads which were in the middle of the town.

As always, they had taken Scary Bones' grey box

with them. They took his grey box everywhere they went because, whenever they needed Scary Bones' help, they only had to call his name and he would pop out of it. And, whenever it was time for him to leave, he would jump back into the box, turn into a golden glow and then disappear.

The grey box was also where the magical piece of Red String slept while it waited for Scary Bones to come back again. It came to life whenever Scary Bones was about to pop out of his box and, when it came to life, it could think, move, fly, grow, shrink; in fact it could do almost anything at all. The Red String really was magical.

Now normally Sasha and Ben only called to Scary Bones when they were in some sort of trouble or other and needed to be rescued. But today the children were going to call into the box, not because they needed Scary Bones to rescue them or to get them out of trouble, but because they wanted him to see where they had come to stay.

'*Scary Bones*,' they called into the grey box. They called very softly so that their Grandma would not hear them, '*Sccaaaarrrrry Bonesssssss, where are you?*'

At first nothing happened, nothing what-so-ever. The grey box just sat there, like it usually did, grey, silent and still. But then they noticed that the Red String, which had been curled up in one of the corners, had started to uncurl itself and was strrreeetttcccchhing and strrreeetttcccchhinggg just like a sleepy cat that had been cat-napping and had just been woken up. As it stretched, they heard the faint rattling of bones, skeleton bones, and a golden glow began to appear in the box. Then, quite suddenly and with one of the quietest of loud wwwhhhooooossssshhhesss's ever to have ever been loud whooshed quietly, Scary Bones popped out of the golden glow looking as happy and as golden as he had ever looked ever.

'*Hoorah, hoorah,*' the children cheered loudly as quietly as anyone can cheer loudly quietly. 'Scary Bones, you're back!' and they laughed and danced so happily around Scary Bones that he began to laugh and dance too. The Red String, which was now fully awake, began to fly around and twirl around them to show that it was very happy too that Scary Bones was back again.

In no time at all Sasha and Ben were so completely out of puff that they had to stop dancing and sit down to recover at least some of their puff. Because, like all skeletons, Scary Bones had nowhere to keep any 'puff' at all, he could have danced on and on for ever and ever and perhaps even longer than that. You see, if you have never had any puff, then you can never run out of it.

'Stop, stop, Scary Bones,' the children laughed. 'Please stop Scary Bones, we are completely out of puff and can't dance for a moment longer.'

Scary Bones laughed too and stopped dancing.

'Well now,' he said, 'where, I wonder, have you brought me to this time? Let me see what I can see,' and he went over to a little window and looked out to see what he could see.

Although they were still getting their puff back, Sasha and Ben stood up and went to look out of the window with Scary Bones.

'This is our Grandma's house,' Sasha said.

'And the town you see is called Wareham,' Ben added.

'And a very nice town it looks too,' Scary Bones said, 'but do you know I see something that is very very strange about it?'

The children looked out of the window this way

and that, and then they looked that way and this, but everything looked perfectly normal to them.

'I can't see anything strange,' said Sasha.

'Nor can I,' said Ben, 'I can't see anything that is strange either.'

'So what do you see that is so strange Scary Bones?' Sasha asked.

'Well,' said Scary Bones, 'it's what I can't see and what I can see that is strange. What I can't see are any children anywhere at all, and what I can see are lots and lots of cats sleeping or dozing here, there and everywhere.'

Sasha and Ben looked out at the town again.

'Scary Bones is right,' said Ben. 'There aren't any children anywhere, but there are lots and lots of cats sleeping and dozing all over the place!'

'I can't see any children either,' said Sasha, 'but there must be some children somewhere because look, down there, by the crossroads,' and she pointed towards the crossroads in the middle of the town. 'See, there are two lollipop ladies and if there are lollipop ladies about, there must be some children about somewhere.'

Ben and Scary Bones looked to where Sasha was pointing and saw that there were indeed two ladies standing at the crossroads and one of them was holding a large school crossing lollipop. They didn't quite look like normal lollipop ladies should look, but they had a lollipop so they had to be lollipop ladies.

The children felt as though they had seen these two ladies before but they couldn't for the life of them remember where. One was long and thin with pointy ears. She was wearing a long purple coat with long tails at the back which nearly touched the ground and a long pointed hat which drooped in the middle. She looked a little bit like a silly penguin. The other one was short and round. She had a long pointed hat that was droopy too but she was wearing a shorter dark green coat with a big leather belt around her round tummy so that she looked like a big plump beetle.

And, although they didn't know quite what it was, Sasha, Ben and Scary Bones felt that there was something very very strange about these two lollipop ladies. For one thing, their lollipop didn't say, '*Stop, Children Crossing*', it just said, '*Stop Children!*' And for another thing, there weren't any children to stop or to cross anywhere. And for a last thing, there were lots and lots of cats sleeping and dozing all around them and all around the town; they were here, there and everywhere. It was all very very strange indeed!

'Well, if anyone will know where all the children are,' said Sasha, 'it will be those two lollipop ladies. I say let's go and ask them.'

'We can't,' said Ben. 'You know that Grandma told us that tonight is Halloween which means that there could be witches and all sorts of strange things happening in Wareham tonight. She said that while it's Halloween we must never ever go out into the town on our own.'

'But we won't be going out on our own,' Sasha said. 'We'll have Scary Bones with us. Come on Ben, don't be such a scaredy scaredy custard.'

Ben was trapped. Sasha always called him this when he tried to be sensible, and if that didn't get him to do what she wanted, she would double dare him to do it. And when she double dared him, he would have to do it anyway. He might as well give in right now.

'Alright,' he said, 'but we'll have to disguise Scary Bones so that no-one will see that he is a skeleton.'

'Don't I have a say in this?' asked Scary Bones.

'No, I'm afraid you don't this time,' said Sasha and turned to Ben. 'He can wear some of your clothes, Ben, and the mask you brought to wear for Halloween.'

'That's a good idea,' said Ben and, in less time than it takes to go from here to there, or even from there to here, Scary Bones looked like any boy anywhere dressed up ready to go to a Halloween party that very night.

'Right, let's go,' said Sasha, 'but we will have to creep out very quietly so that Grandma doesn't hear us.'

'That means you will have to stop your bones from rattling Scary Bones, can you do that?'

Scary Bones nodded his head and smiled nervously although the children couldn't see that he was nervous because his face was completely hidden by the mask.

They crept very slowly and very quietly down the stairs. *Creep, creep, crreeeeak, creep, rattle, creep, crrreeeeak, creep, rattle, creep....* Sasha opened the door, as quietly as she could, *click-clack, ccrreeeeeeaakk,* and then closed it very quietly, *ccreeeeeeeaakk, click-clack.*

They went out onto the street and set off towards the middle of the town to find the two very strange lollipop ladies. And as they walked towards the crossroads, following right behind them skipping and slithering along as happy as it could be, was the magical piece of Red String.

Chapter 2

When they reached the crossroads in the middle of the town, the two lollipop ladies were still standing where the children and Scary Bones had seen them from the window. As they got nearer to the two ladies, they could see the ladies' faces more clearly.

The tall thin one had a long droopy wet nose with hairs sprouting from it. The short round one's nose was short and round with two big warts on it which jumped about like two puppies in a bag when she wriggled it. Both of them had large round eyes which were a very bright green and shone like a black cat's eyes on a dark black night.

'Eh eh eh eeehh,' the two ladies cackled as the children came towards them, 'eh, eh, eh eh-eh-eh-eeeehh.'

'And vhat do you think ve have here Vendy?' the tall thin one said to the small round one and she rubbed her hands together so that her long bony fingers squirmed around each other like a nest of snakes.

'I think ve have three wery lovely children here Walerie,' the short one replied, 'the sort of wery lovely children anyone vould like to take home vith them,' and the two ladies laughed and cackled together.

Their cackling made the children and Scary Bones feel quite nervous but they tried hard not to let the two ladies see that they were nervous.

'Hello,' said Ben in the bravest voice he could find, 'my name is Ben and this is my sister Sasha, and this is our best friend Scallywag.' Ben called Scary Bones 'Scallywag' because, in their first adventure together, a grumpy lady called Mrs Grumble had called Scary Bones a 'scallywag'.

'Ve are wery pleased to meet you all, I'm sure,' the tall thin one replied with a smile of long yellow pointy teeth. It was a little like the smile of a friendly crocodile. 'My name is Walerie and this is my friend Vendy.'

The short round one seemed to smile at them too but her mouth was too little and too round for them to be absolutely sure.

'Walerie and Vendy?' Sasha said in suprise. She had never heard of such names and so she asked, 'Are you really called Walerie and Vendy?'

'No, no' the short one said. 'Ve are Walerie and Vendy. I am Vendy and this is Walerie.

'But that's what I said,' said Sasha. 'Walerie and Vendy.'

'Oh no you didn't,' the thin one said, 'you said Walerie and Vendy, and ve said ve are Walerie and Vendy.'

Scary Bones realised what the problem might be and whispered to the children, 'I think that they get their Wees mixed up with their Vubbleyous.'

Although they were still very nervous Sasha and Ben could not help laughing. 'Yes, that's it, they get their Wees mixed up with their Vubbleyous!'

'Yes, let's see if you are right Scallywag,' said Ben and then, speaking to the tall thin one, he said, 'so you must be Valerie.' Then he turned to the short round one and said, 'and you must be Wendy.'

The two ladies were delighted. 'Yes, yes. That's vhat ve said, Walerie and Vendy. Now vhat can ve do for you three wery lovely children?' and they rubbed their hands and stared at the children and Scary Bones.

'Well,' said Sasha, 'we were wondering why there are no children in Wareham. Where have they all gone?'

The tall thin one, Valerie, stroked her long hairy chin to show that she was thinking as hard as anyone with a long hairy chin could ever think. 'So you vere vondering vere all the children in Vareham have gone. So vere ve, vern't ve Vendy?'

'Yes ve vere, Walerie' the short round one called Wendy replied. 'Ve vere vondering the very same thing. Vould you like us to help you look for them?'

Although Scary Bones was shaking his head towards the children so much that his teeth rattled, Ben replied, 'Oh yes please, that would be very very kind of you.'

'Oh yes,' said Valerie. 'Ve are wery wery kind old vitc...' She stopped and started again. 'Ve are wery wery kind old ladies, don't you know?'

'Perhaps ve vill find the children are playing by the river or under the bridge,' Wendy said. 'Perhaps ve vill look down by the river first.'

'Well we didn't see them there when we looked out from our Grandma's house but I suppose that it's worth a try,' said Sasha.

'Vell, off ve go then,' said Valerie. 'Come on Vendy and don't forget your lollipop.'

'Oh yes,' Wendy replied, 'now vere did I put it? Ah, yes, here it is!' and she reached into a tiny little pocket and pulled a full size *'Children Crossing'* lollipop out of it! Wendy did this as though there was nothing unusual about pulling such a large lollipop out of such a tiny pocket.

The children, however, were very surprised indeed because they knew that there couldn't be such a tiny pocket anywhere in the whole wide world that would be big enough to have a *'Children Crossing'* lollipop inside it. It was as if it were magic.

'Right, off ve go again,' said Valerie and they all set off down towards the bridge over the river with the Red String slithering along behind them. And following them all, a little behind the Red String, there trotted every cat that could meow or purr in the whole town of Wareham. Every cat that had been sleeping or dozing was now wide awake and was following them along the road.

As they passed by the shops which were on either side of the road, Scary Bones noticed something that was a little more than strange, in fact it was very very peculiar. The big glass windows of the shops were behaving just like big mirrors so that Scary Bones could see himself, the Red String and the children in the windows as they walked past. In some of the biggest big windows he could even see all of the cats too.

What Scary Bones found a little more than strange, in fact very very peculiar, was that, no matter how hard he tried, he could not see Valerie and Wendy in the windows. It was as if Valerie and Wendy weren't walking along with them at all. It was as if they were invisible! Behind his mask and inside the clothes he was wearing, Scary Bones was beginning to turn blue and, as you know, when skeletons turn blue, it means that they are frightened!

As the children and Scary Bones got closer to the bridge the cats began meowing and caterwauling, and the closer the children and Scary Bones got to the bridge, the louder the cats meowed and caterwauled. Then the cats began to run around them as if they were trying to stop the children and Scary Bones from getting to the bridge. Valerie and Wendy tried to chase the cats away by waving their lollipops at them but the cats kept coming back.

'What on earth is the matter with the cats?' Sasha asked, 'I have never seen so many cats behaving in such a strange way.'

'Vait until ve are on the bridge, then ve have a vay to frighten them avay,' said Valerie. As soon as they reached the bridge, Valerie and Wendy suddenly grabbed a cat each and threw it over the bridge into the river. Ssssspllaaaaassshhhhhh, sssspllaaaasssshhh. When the other cats saw this they turned around and, with their tails pointing straight up to the sky, ran back towards the town as fast as their cattie legs could carry them.

'Wery good, Walerie,' said Wendy, 'that has frightened them all avay.'

'Ohhh, that's a terrible thing to do!' Ben shouted at Valerie and Wendy. 'Cats don't like water and they may not be able to swim. They could drown!'

Sasha, Ben and Scary Bones ran to the bridge and looked down into the river. The two cats were splashing about trying to breathe and blow water out of their mouths, noses and ears all at the same time.

'They are going to drown,' Sasha called to the two ladies. 'You've got to save them!'

'Oh, wery vell. I have a little werse that may help them,' the one called Valerie said. She pointed one of her long fingers towards one of the cats splashing about in the river and said,

'Cat in the vater, O vhat luck,
You vent in as a cat and
You come out as a ....duck!'

She snapped her fingers, *click*, there was a small puff of smoke followed by a '*quack, quack*' and they saw that the cat had turned into a duck!

Then Valerie pointed her long finger at the other cat which was still splashing about in the water and snapped her fingers, *click*. There was another puff of smoke, and that cat turned into a duck too. Then, quack quacking as loudly as any two quack quacking ducks could ever quack quack, the two ducks swam to the river bank and waddled up and out of the water.

'You've turned the two cats into ducks!' Ben cried. 'You can't do that, they're cats, not ducks. It's not allowed to turn cats into ducks, it's cruel.'

'Vell, vell, vell,' said Wendy. 'Aren't you the little bossy boots? Oh wery vell, let's see vhat ve can do vith another little werse.' She pointed two of her stubby little fingers at the two ducks and said,

17

'Ducks have feathers, cats have fur,
Ducks quack quack and cats purr purr,
And so little ducks it's time right now,
To stop your quack quacking and
Go meow meow meow meow'.

As she finished her poem, she snapped her fingers and there were two small puffs of smoke followed by 'meow meow meow'. When the smoke blew away on the wind, the two ducks had been turned back into two cats again! With their tails pointing straight up to the sky the two cats ran off to join the other cats who were all waiting a little way off up the road.

Now most children would have been very, very surprised to see cats turned into ducks, or even ducks turned back into cats. For Sasha and Ben, however, because of the things that had happened to them since they had met Scary Bones, Sasha and Ben were not surprised one tiny little bit. Well, perhaps the tiniest of tiny little tiny bits.

'How did you do that?' they asked Valerie and Wendy with the tiniest of tiny little bits of tiny surprise.

'Do vhat vhen?' the two ladies replied and smiled their strange smiles as though nothing unusual had happened at all.

The children were just about to ask again when there was a great meowing and caterwauling from the big crowds of cats who were watching them from nearby. The cats' meowing and caterwauling was so loud that, even if the children had tried to ask again, Valerie and Wendy would have never heard what they said.

Scary Bones and the children wondered why the cats were making such a noise and looked towards them. As soon as they looked at the cats, the cats began waving their paws and signalling to them as if they wanted Scary Bones and the children to go to them. Scary Bones also felt that the cats were trying to tell them that they were in great danger if they stayed with the two ladies. The more he thought about the two strange ladies, the more he thought that they might do something terrible to him and the children.

Behind his mask and inside his clothes, Scary Bones began turning from being just blue to being very blue, and as you know, when skeletons turn from blue to very blue, it means they are not just frightened, they are very frightened!

Sasha and Ben, however, were too puzzled by the way the cats were behaving to think about anything else.

'What on earth is the matter with the cats?' Ben said.

'I think that they think that ve have something they vant, like a little mouse perhaps,' Wendy said and she pulled a little mouse out of her pocket. Holding the mouse by its tail, she held it up so that all of the cats could see it and then she dropped it to the ground. As soon as it landed on the ground, the little mouse ran around squeaking like a little piglet that has lost its mother. '*Squeaky squeaky, squeaky.*'

Then Wendy pulled out another mouse, and then another, and then another. She went on and on pulling mice out of her pocket and dropping them to the ground. Once they were on the ground every single one ran around squeak squeaking like a little piglet that had lost its mother.

Then Valerie began pulling mice out of her pockets and dropping them to the ground. Soon there were hundreds and hundreds of mice running around and squeak squeaking here, there and everywhere.

Now, if there's one thing that cats cannot resist chasing, it is mice, particularly mice that run around squeak squeaking. They just can't help it. They just have to chase after mice that run around squeak squeaking. And now, here, right in front of their cattie eyes, there were more mice than anyone has ever seen since the whole wide world began, and perhaps even longer than that, running around squeak squeaking.

The cats could not resist and they did just what every cat has done ever since the very first cat ever purr purred or meowed meowed. They began to chase towards the mice. And, when the mice saw the cats chasing towards them, they ran off into the town as fast as their little mousey legs could carry them squeak squeaking even more loudly than they were squeak squeaking before. The cats chased after them and very soon there were no chasing cats or squeak squeaking mice to be seen or heard here, there or anywhere at all.

The whole of Wareham town had become strangely silent. In the silence Sasha, Ben, Scary Bones and the Red String began to think about where they were and what was happening around them. They realised that they were all alone on a bridge with two very strange ladies who could turn cats into ducks and ducks into cats, and probably lots of other silly or nasty things too.

They realised, too, that it was getting very dark. The sun had gone from the sky and a big bright silvery moon had taken its place. In the black sky above them there was not a single star to be seen and a strong wind whistled and howled around their ears and tugged at their hair and clothes.

And then they remembered! They remembered that their Grandma had told them that tonight was Halloween that there could be witches and all sorts of strange things happening in Wareham town tonight. Halloween, the one night in the whole year when all sorts of witches and wizards come out to play and to torment the innocent!

Behind his mask and inside his clothes, Scary Bones was turning from being very blue to being very very blue, and as you know, when skeletons are very very frightened, they turn from being very blue to being very very blue! And now even Sasha and Ben were very very frightened too!

The MANY CATS of WAREHAM

Big cats and small cats
Thin cats and fat cats,
Hairy cats and scary cats
Furry cats and purry cats,
Sleepy cats and creepy cats,
Dig-a-hole cats and climb-a-pole cats,
Peaceful cats and wild cats,
Lappy cats and happy cats,
Stumpy cats and grumpy cats,
Fireside cats and green eyed cats,
Day time cats and night time cats,
Lost again cats and found again cats,
Up on the roof cats and very aloof cats,
Sooty black cats and snowy white cats,
Meow cats and don't bother me now cats,
Friskery cats and whiskery cats,
Tabby cats and McNabby cats,
Cheshire cats and Marmalade cats,
All sorts of loverly cats,
And every one an aristo-cat.

Chapter 3

The children, Scary Bones and the Red String were all very very frightened. They were all alone on a bridge on a very dark night with two very strange ladies who were able to turn things into what they should not be and things that should not be into things that they should be. Or something like that anyway.

The ladies seemed to be much taller and bigger now than when the children and Scary Bones had first met them. The ladies looked stranger too. Their bright green eyes were shining even more brightly and their droopy hats had become completely undroopified. Now their hats were stiff and round, and hard, and shiny, and with a sharp point at the top. They looked just like the sort of hats that witches wear! Scary Bones, Sasha, Ben and even the Red String were now more than just very very frightened. Now they were all very very very frightened!

Although his teeth were chattering and his eyes were double-popping, Ben managed to speak to the two ladies. In a voice that quivered and quavered like a screechy violin, he said to them,

'You are not wicked witches, ….. are you?'

'Vicked vitches? Vendy and I?' said Valerie, 'Vhat ever made you vonder such as thing? No, no, ve cannot be vicked vitches because look, ve do not even have a cat.'

'And you see,' said Wendy, 'you can't be a vitch if you don't have a cat, and every cat in Vareham already belongs to a vitch somevere.'

'Every cat that is but you my three little dears,' Valerie said with an evil smile.

'But we're not three cats,' Sasha said angrily, 'we are three children.'

At that very moment the great bell of Wareham Church began to ring out.

'Yes my dear. Yes you are three children, but vait just a moment for us to see vot ve can do about that,' Wendy said and she and Valerie began to dance around them chanting a poem as they danced and the great bell rang out.

> *'Ding dong bell,*
> *Put these children in a spell,*
> *And the spell that says that*
> *They vill each become a .... CAT.'*

As they finished their chant, they pointed and snapped their fingers at Scary Bones and the children. There was a claaaaaaaaaap of thunder, a FLASH of lightening and two little puffs of smoke puffed up from the bridge. When the wind had

27

blown the puffs of smoke away, where Sasha and Ben had been standing, there were now two very strange looking cats.

Valerie and Wendy had used a magic spell to turn the children into two cats. But because they had mixed up a wee with a voubleyou when they chanted their spell, it had not worked as well as it should have. The problem was that not every bit of Sasha and Ben had turned into a cat. Nearly all of them had but not every last bit because, although Sasha and Ben were cats everywhere else, they still had their own faces!

Another thing that seemed to have gone wrong was that Scary Bones was still standing right where he had been when the magic spell was cast. He was still a whole skeleton and he was still very very blue behind his mask. The Red String was still a Red String too but it was so frightened that it had wrapped itself around Scary Bones' leg.

The two ladies were very surprised to see Scary Bones had not been turned into a cat and was still standing there in front of them with the Red String wrapped around his leg.

'Vat has happened?' Wendy said pointing at Scary Bones. 'You should be a cat now. Ve should have three cats but ve have only two cats.'

'Don't vorry,' Valerie said, 'Ve only need two cats, one for you and one for me. And now that ve both have a cat, ve can become proper vitches. Ve vill be able to fly with the other vitches to visit the vicked vizard and be turned into proper vicked vitches.' And the two ladies cackled loudly, 'Eh eh eh-eheh, eh eh eh-eheh.'

'But look,' Wendy said pointing to the sky, 'it's time for us to go!'

Against the bright silver circle of the moon, whole flocks of black witches could be seen flying through the black night on their broomsticks away from Wareham town. And on every broomstick, behind every witch, was a cat.

Valerie and Wendy put their lollipops between their legs and sat on them as if they were witches' broomsticks. Valerie grabbed the cat with Sasha's face and Wendy grabbed the cat with Ben's face and put them behind them on their lollipops. Then, with a shout of, 'hold on wery tightly cats and avay ve go,' they whoooossshhhed up into the sky on their lollipops and flew away after the other witches.

The cats that had been Sasha and Ben were helpless and, as Valerie and Wendy flew away with them, their faces shouted back to Scary Bones and the Red String,

'HHHHHEEEEEEEEEEELLLLPPPPP……'

The shouts for help from the two cats who had been Sasha and Ben faded into the distance and Scary Bones and the Red String were left all alone on the bridge. Although Scary Bones didn't know it, he had been saved from Valerie and Wendy's spell to turn him into a cat because he was a skeleton. You see, witches' spells just don't work on skeletons. So no matter how much Valerie and Wendy had chanted their spell, or how much they had pointed and snapped their fingers, because Scary Bones was a skeleton, none of their magic spells could have ever worked on him.

Scary Bones was beginning to wonder if the spell had worked on him, would he have changed into a skeleton cat or into a full furry cat? He was having these thoughts when the Red String flew up to him. It stretched itself out so that it became long and straight and then it spread out its strands at one end so that it looked just like a red broomstick. Then it floated in the air, just like a witch's broomstick, except that it was red.

Because Scary Bones was very sad at what had happened to his friends, he had turned to grey but, when he saw the Red String behaving like a witch's broomstick, he turned to a bright purple. Purple is the colour skeletons turn to when they are feeling angry or very brave, and Scary Bones was feeling both very angry and very brave now.

'You are right,' he shouted to the Red String. 'It's no use feeling sorry for ourselves, we must be brave and go to the rescue of our two friends, Sasha and Ben!'

With that, he threw off his clothes and mask and jumped onto the red string just as if it was a witch's broomstick and together they whoosshhed up into the sky to fly after Valerie and Wendy and all of the other witches.

As Scary Bones and the Red String flew along they could see the witches flying along in front of them and that they were flying towards the black shadow of a ruined castle. It was Corfe Castle which is not very far from Wareham town and is so old that lots of it have fallen down. What is left of the castle stands on the very top of a steep hill that looks like a giant pimple. Soon all of the witches were flying around and around the castle.

Then, quite suddenly, the witches swooped down to land at the bottom of the steep hill. As soon as they had landed, they got off their broomsticks, stood in a big circle and threw their cats into the middle of the circle. The cats ran around meowing and caterwauling and trying to escape from the circle but the witches beat them back with their broomsticks.

Valerie and Wendy were the last to land but when they put the cats with Sasha and Ben's faces into the circle the other witches began to laugh and cackle as loudly as any witches ever have cackled loudly. 'Ehhheee ehhheeehee eeehheeee'.

'Look at the silly cats,' the witches cackled and hooted. 'Look at the silly faces on those silly cats, ehheeehhhee eehhheeeehee eeehhhheeeeheeee.'

Now when Scary Bones and the Red String saw Valerie and Wendy land with the other witches, they landed too. They landed near to a clump of trees and then hid themselves among the trees so that, while they could see what the witches were doing, the witches would not be able to see them.

A noise noisier than the nosiest noisy noise that has ever noised noisily arose all around the castle. All of the cats were wailing and caterwauling. All of the witches were laughing and cackling at the cats with Sasha and Ben's faces. And, in all of this noise, the Sasha and Ben cats were shouting more loudly than they had ever shouted in their whole lives even before they had been turned into cats.

'SCARY BONES, SCARY BONES, PLEASE SAVE US, PLEASE COME AND SAVE US FROM THE WITCHES. HEEEELLLLPPPPP..'

Scary Bones and the Red String were watching and listening from the trees but there was nothing they could do. Although Scary Bones knew that witches are frightened of skeletons, there were just too many witches for them all to be frightened by one little skeleton and a piece of Red String. There was nothing they could do to rescue their friends. It seemed that, no matter what the witches planned to do with them, for Sasha and Ben there was ….. NO ESCAPE!

Chapter 4

The noisy noises from the cats' meowing, wailing and caterwauling, and from the witches' laughing and cackling, and from the Sasha and Ben cats' cries for help became louder and louder. Then, quite suddenly, out from the castle, a booming voice that boomed more boomier than the boomiest booming voice has ever boom boomed, boomed above all of the noisy noises.

'SSSSSSILLLEEEEEENNNNNNCCCCCE!'

The witches stopped their laughing and cackling and the cats stopped their wailing and caterwauling. The only noisy thing to be heard in the silence was the Sasha and Ben cats' cries for help.

'SCARY BONES, SCARY BONES, PLEASE SAVE US! PLEASE COME AND SAVE US! HHHEEEEELLLLLPPPPPPP.'

'Shush, shush!' Valerie and Wendy shushed to the Sasha and Ben cats to shush. 'It is the vicked Vizard of Corfe Castle. He has told everyone to be silent and he must be obeyed. Look there he is coming to life now!' and they pointed up to the Castle. The Castle now seemed to have the eyes and shape of a giant Wizard's head.

'WHAT IS ALL THIS NOISY NOISE ABOUT?' boomed the Wizard's voice, 'AND WHERE IS THIS 'SCARY BONES' THEY CALL FOR? BRING HIM TO ME NOW!

The witches looked around and saw Scary Bones and the Red String hiding in the trees.

'There he is,' they all shouted. 'Capture him, capture him!' and they began running towards Scary Bones and the Red String. There seemed to be no escape for Scary Bones but then he noticed that the witches didn't have their broomsticks with them. He got onto the Red String again as if it were a broomstick and waited until the witches were so close that they could nearly touch him.

Then, at the very last moment, he shouted to the Red String, 'Right, broooomm, brooooooomm, let's gooooooooohhhhh!' The Red String broooommm brooooommed and whooshed up into the sky with

Scary Bones sitting on it and whooshed as fast as it could whoosh back towards Wareham town.

By the time the witches had run back to get their broomsticks, Scary Bones and the Red String had completely disappeared into the night sky.

'YOU HAVE FAILED ME!' the Wizard's voice boomed, 'YOU WILL ALL PAY FOR YOUR FAILURE. NOW, WHO BROUGHT THOSE TWO STRANGE CATS HERE TONIGHT?'

The witches all looked and pointed at Valerie and Wendy and so the wicked Wizard knew that it was them.

'VALERIE AND WENDY, WHAT HAVE YOU GOT TO SAY FOR YOURSELVES?' he boomed.

'Ve say that ve are wery sorry,' they said. 'Ve vant to be proper vitches so wery wery much, and these vere the only cats ve could find in the vhole of Vareham.' They didn't want to tell the Wizard that their magic spell had not worked as well as a proper witch's magic spell would have worked.

'WELL NOW,' the Wizard boomed, 'BECAUSE OF WHAT YOU HAVE DONE, YOU WILL NEVER EVER BECOME PROPER WITCHES. LOCK THEM AND THE TWO STRANGE CATS IN THE DUNGEON INSIDE THE HILL WHERE THEY WILL STAY FOR EVER AND EVER!'

As the Wizard stopped booming, a door opened in the side of the hill and the witches threw Valerie, Wendy and the Sasha and Ben cats through the door and banged it shut.

'NOW,' the Wizard boomed to the witches, 'GET TO YOUR WORK. YOUR WORK MUST BE FINISHED BEFORE THE SUN RISES ONCE MORE IN THE EAST!'

The witches gathered into a circle around the cats again and began to chant :

'There's wicked Wizard's work to be done,
It's not work for cats so cats …… be gone
And become the children you once were,
Again to work, no more to ……. purr.'

There was a FLASH of bright lightning and a clap of loud thunder. The witches pointed at the cats and snapped their fingers. Inside the circle, where all the cats had been there were now little puffs of smoke everywhere. And when the puffs of smoke had blown away on the wind, every single one of the cats had been turned into a boy or into a girl.

The witches began to sing and, as they sang, they prodded and hit the children with their broomsticks. This is the song they were singing:

> '*Now every Jack and Jill*
> *Must carry stones to the top of the hill,*
> *To rebuild the Wizard's den, and then*
> *He will rule the world........ again!*'

The witches made the strongest of the children pick up heavy blocks of stone that had fallen down from the castle. They made the children put the blocks on their shoulders and carry them to the top of the hill. At the top of the hill, other children were being made to use the blocks to rebuild Corfe Castle. And if any boy or girl slipped or stumbled, spoke or grumbled, the witches beat them very hard with their broom sticks.

Through a crack in the door to their dungeon inside the hill, the cats who were Sasha and Ben, and the two strange ladies, Valerie and Wendy, watched as the witches used the children as slaves to rebuild Corfe Castle.

'I wonder why are the witches making the children rebuild the castle?' Ben said.

'Vell, you see,' said Valerie, 'long long ago a vicked vizard, the maker of all vitches, vanted to show that he vas the most powerful vicked Vizard in the vhole vide verld. So he turned himself into a castle, this castle, Corfe Castle. But it vas a wery silly thing to do because, just as he did it, a block of stone fell off the castle. Now, because he had a piece missing, he lost some of his magic and he couldn't turn himself back into a vizard.'

'And,' Wendy said, 'vhen even more of the castle fell down, the less and less powerful his magic became. And now, his magic is so veak that it is only at Halloween that he has any magical powers at all.'

'But,' Valerie said, 'vhen the vitches and children have rebuilt the castle and every stone is back in place, the Vizard vill get all of his magic powers back. He vill be able to turn himself back to the powerful vicked Vizard he once vas and he vill rule the vorld again.'

'And he vill make lots and lots more vitches,' said Vendy, 'that is vhy ve came tonight, ve vanted to be made into proper vitches.'

Although Sasha and Ben were more like cats than children now, everything became clear to them. The reason why there were no children in Wareham was because the witches were using them to rebuild Corfe Castle. The witches were making the children work at night so that no-one would find out what they were doing.

So that the children could not tell their parents or anyone else what was happening, the witches turned the children into cats during the day time. And because they had worked so hard as children all through the night, the cats were so tired that they couldn't do anything except doze and sleep all day.

There was nothing, however, that Sasha and Ben could do to help the other children or even to help themselves. Apart from their faces, they were two cats now and they were the Wizard's prisoners locked in a dungeon in the hill beneath the castle. The only thing they could do was to run around in circles with their tails straight up in the air and that did no good for anyone anywhere at all!

'What do you think the Wizard will do with us?' the Sasha and Ben cats asked Valerie and Wendy.

41

'Ve don't know,' Valerie replied. 'But ve do know that he is a wery vicked Vizard and vill vant something wery wery vicked to happen to us all.'

'Vhatever happens,' said Wendy, 'Ve are wery wery sorry for vhat ve have done and if ve ever get out of here, ve promise never to vant to be vitches ever again or do anything that is wery wery vrong.'

'Yes, ve promise ve vill be the wery wery nice lollipop ladies that ve used to be,' said Valerie.

'Well I'm very pleased to hear that,' the Sasha cat said, 'because although I don't know where he is or what he is doing right now, I know that Scary Bones will come back and rescue us somehow.'

'Well I hope that you are right,' the Ben cat said, 'because time is running out very fast for us.'

After whooooshing away from the witches Scary Bones and the Red String had flown back to Wareham Town. They had landed in the giant graveyard behind the church and Scary Bones had sat down on a big gravestone.

'Now let me think what I can think,' he said and tapped his head although that he knew that it was completely empty inside. The Red String tried to help him by making itself into the shape of a

question mark which Scary Bones knew meant
'THINK, Scary Bones, THINK!'

'OK,' said Scary Bones, 'I will think as hard as I can think,' and he put on his best '*I'm thinking very hard*' look to show the Red String that he was thinking very hard. He even stroked his bony chin.

'Now, how can we save our two friends? There are too many witches for us to fight or to frighten, so what can we do? Mmmmmm. I can't think of a single thing but I do know that if we don't think of a single thing and do something, then Sasha and Ben will stay as two cats locked inside the hill beneath Corfe castle for ever and ever, and perhaps even longer than that.'

The thought of losing his friends for ever turned Scary Bones to a grey that was as grey as a grey can be and still be grey. The Red String knew that this meant that Scary Bones was as sad as sad can be and so stopped being a question mark and wrapped itself around Scary Bone's shoulders to comfort him. But it knew too that there was nothing they could do. They knew that for Sasha and Ben, there was ...... NO ESCAPE!

Chapter 5

Scary Bones was as sad and as grey as he could ever be. His friends Sasha and Ben had been turned into cats and were the prisoners of an evil Wizard and his wicked witches and he couldn't think of anything he could do to save them.

Now, as you probably know, because they don't have anywhere to store their teardrops, skeletons can't cry. But now, because Scary Bones was so very sad, the strangest of things was happening. There, slowly rolling down Scary Bones' cheek bone, was a silver pearl which is what skeletons have in place of teardrops. It rolled down his cheek bone and over his chin bone and then fell onto his chest bones. As it fell and bounced from chest bone to chest bone, it tinkled like a small bell. 'Tinkle... tinkle.... tinkle.... tinkle.'

When the pearl teardrop fell from his bottom-most chest bone, it fell onto the grave stone with a 'ding ding ding'. The 'ding ding ding' dinged and echoed all around the silent grave yard like a hundred ding ding dinging doorbells. Then, slowly but surely in the dark silence, rattling noises began coming from here, there and everywhere all around the graveyard. The rattling noises got louder and louder and then, as if from

nowhere, hundreds and hundreds of bright silver
skeletons popped up here, there and everywhere
all over the graveyard.

'Did you ding ding ding a bell for me?' one
skeleton asked another.

'No,' said the other, 'I thought that it was you
that had ding ding dinged a bell for me.'

'Well,' they asked each other, 'who under the
earth ding ding dinged a bell for both of us then?'

And all over the graveyard skeletons were asking
each other the same questions. But Scary Bones
was so sad that he didn't notice, or perhaps he
just didn't care, that there were skeletons all
around him now. One of the skeletons, however,
noticed Scary Bones sitting all alone on the big
gravestone and looking very very sad. The
skeleton went across to Scary Bones to find out
what was the matter with him.

When the skeleton looked at Scary Bones he saw the little silver pearl teardrop which had fallen on to the gravestone. The skeleton picked it up and looked at it very closely.

'This looks to me,' he said, 'very much like a skeleton's teardrop and skeletons can only cry teardrops when they are very very sad or even sadder than that. I think that this teardrop came from you and when it fell it made the ding ding dinging that we all heard. Now, tell us what is the matter and we may be able to help you.'

The skeletons all gathered around Scary Bones to listen to why he was so very very sad. He told them about his friends, Sasha and Ben, and how they had almost been turned into cats by two strange ladies called Valerie and Wendy. He told them how he and the Red String had followed hundreds of witches as they flew with their cats to Corfe Castle, and how a monster wicked Wizard was trapped inside it.

'And where are your friends who have been turned into cats now?' the skeletons asked.

'The wicked Wizard has locked them up inside the steep hill beneath Corfe Castle for ever and ever, and perhaps even longer that that.'

'He can't do that,' the skeletons cried. 'Even wicked Wizards are not allowed to lock anyone up for ever and ever, or perhaps even longer than that.'

'But he has done it,' said Scary Bones, 'and there's nothing that we can do about that.'

'Well, we'll see about that,' the skeletons all shouted. 'You must show us the way to Corfe Castle and we'll see about that!'

'Right,' Scary Bones said to the Red String, 'you know what to do.'

The Red String stretched itself out so that it became long and straight. Then it spread out its strands at one end so that it looked just like a red broomstick again and, when it did, Scary Bones sat on it.

'Right,' Scary Bones shouted to the skeletons, 'get ready for takeoff because we are going to fly to Corfe Castle to rescue our friends!' Scary Bones knew, you see, that because Skeletons don't have a body, they are so light that they can all fly.

The skeletons cheered and cheered and got ready for takeoff.

'Is everyone ready,' Scary Bones shouted.

'YEEESSSSS,' all of the other skeletons shouted back to him.

'Right, then off we go!' Scary Bones cried and the Red String wwwhhhooooooosssssshhhhed up into the sky with all of the other skeletons whooshing up right behind them. Scary Bones, of course, could have whooshed along with the other skeletons, but he liked riding on the Red String as if it were a broomstick.

As Scary Bones and the skeletons got near to the castle they could see that the children had nearly finished rebuilding it. There was just one block of stone left to be put in place. And although he didn't quite know why, Scary Bones knew that they had to stop that last block of stone being put into place.

'Action stations, action stations,' he shouted. 'Enemy straight ahead. Good luck everybody!'

The Red String and Scary Bones dived towards the castle so that the silver moon was behind them. They did this so that the witches would not see them until they were almost at the castle.

The skeletons dived down after them and were going so fast they sounded just like jet aeroplanes. Phhhiissssshhhhoooooo, phhhiissssshhhhoooooo,

Phhhiisssssshhhhooooooooooooooooooooo............

It was the Wizard who saw them first. 'LOOK OUT, LOOK OUT,' he boomed. 'THERE ARE SKELETONS ABOUT!'

Now this was a very silly thing for the Wizard to boom out because, as everyone knows, witches are very afraid of skeletons. This is because skeletons do not like witches one little bit and because, as every proper witch knows, their magic spells simply don't work on skeletons.

The witches looked up and saw the skeletons in their scariest silver coming straight towards them. The skeletons began to make the scariest of their scariest scary noises to frighten the witches.

'*OoooOooooOOooooooooo, OOOoooOOOooooo , OOOooooOOO*'ooooooooooooo ....

With so many scary silver skeletons coming towards them making such scary noises, the witches were very very frightened. In fact they were so frightened that they stopped beating the children and jumped onto their broomsticks and flew off in all directions away from the castle to escape.

The Wizard's voice boomed out from within the castle again, 'STOP, STOP, I COMMAND YOU TO STOP AND COME BACK TO DEFEND ME AND REBUILD THE CASTLE!'

But there were so many scary skeletons that the witches were so frightened that they didn't stop and they didn't come back. Instead they kept flying away as fast as they could but, no matter how fast they flew, or where they flew, or how much they dived or turned, the skeletons kept flying right behind them.

The Wizard's voice boomed out more loudly and angrily than it had ever boomed angrily before. 'YOU HAVE FAILED ME AGAIN. YOU ARE COWARDS ONE AND ALL AND FOR THAT YOU MUST PAY THE PENALTY!'

As he boomed out the words, there was a clap of rolling thunder and FLASHES of lightning FLASHED all over the sky. The lightening FLASHES struck the wooden handles of the witches' broomsticks and split them apart. When their broomsticks split apart, the witches couldn't fly and they were sent crashing to the ground. As they fell they each let out a bloodcurdling scream.

'AAAAAAAhhhhhhhhhhgggggggghhhhhhh........' Bump!

Then, whenever and wherever the witches landed, their broken broomsticks fell like spears into the ground right next to them. The broomsticks stuck deep into the ground so that they pointed up to the sky like the trunks of trees.

Then the strangest of things happened. The broomsticks began to grow branches around the witches so quickly that the witches could not escape from them. Then, from the branches, there grew shiny green leaves which twisted and turned as if in pain from the sharp needles which sprang out at their tips. The leaves covered the trees so thickly that no-one, not even a witch, could touch any of the trees without being pricked and spiked by the spiky leaves.

Now, as you may know, a proper witch's broomstick is always made from the wood of a Holly tree and now, on every spot where a witch and a broomstick had landed, there was a holly tree growing. And within every holly tree a witch was trapped by its tangled branches and spiking leaves.

'NOW,' boomed the Wizard, 'AS I AM TRAPPED INSIDE THIS CASTLE, SO YOU WILL BE TRAPPED FOREVER INSIDE A HOLLY TREE!'

As he boomed his evil spell, each Holly tree began to swallow up the witch trapped within its branches and spiky leaves. Soon, all the witches had been swallowed up by the trees and had become part of the trees themselves. The witches have never been able to escape from inside the trees because, whenever they try to escape, the sharp spiky leaves of the holly trees drive them back. And so to this very day, a witch is still trapped inside every holly tree.

But even so, as Halloween and witches' night gets near, the witches try their hardest to escape from the holly trees. They try and try but the spiky prickly needles on the leaves drive them back and prick their hands so much that they bleed. And when they bleed, their red blood turns the green berries that grow on holly trees into the bright red berries we see on all holly trees after Halloween night has passed.

And do you know that from that day to this, many people believe that a Holly tree can protect us all from wicked witches? But, although that may be true, there is still a danger from the witches trapped inside holly trees because the beautiful bright red berries that grow on the trees are very very poisonous and should never ever be eaten. And why do you think they are so very very poisonous? It is because they have been coloured by a wicked witch's blood!

Chapter 6

The Wizard began to realise that in his silly fit of silly temper he had done something very silly. Without his witches to help him he was alone and helpless. He wished that he had not punished his witches so harshly but it was too late to do anything about that now. His only hope was to get the children to release him from the castle by replacing that last stone block at the very top of the castle.

Using his most frightening boom he boomed out to the children, 'KEEP WORKING MY CHILDREN, YOUR WORK WILL SOON BE DONE. JUST ONE MORE BLOCK TO SEAL MY CROWN AND YOU WILL ALL GO HOME TO WAREHAM TOWN, TO YOUR HOMES, TO YOUR FAMILIES AND TO YOUR FRIENDS!'

The children, who had stopped working to watch the skeletons chasing the witches away, were still so frightened that without thinking they set to work again. The Wizard had told them that all that they had to do was to place that one last block on the top of his castle and they could all go home to their families and friends, and they believed him.

They passed the last stone block from one to the other, then up and up the castle walls and up and up to the highest tower.

'THAT'S THE WAY, MY GOOD CHILDREN,' the Wizard boomed, 'QUICKLY REPLACE THE LAST BLOCK OF STONE, THEN THIS VERY NIGHT YOU WILL ALL GO HOME!'

From within their prison inside the hill the cats with Sasha and Ben's faces watched in horror. They knew that when the last block was put in place the castle would be complete again and the Wizard would be able to release himself from the spell that had locked him inside the castle.

'What can we do to stop them?' the Ben cat cried.

The Sasha cat turned to Valerie and Wendy who were feeling very very sorry for themselves and for the bad things they had done. 'Can't you do anything to help us?' she said, 'a magic spell or something? After all you were very near to becoming proper witches yourselves.'

'Vell, ve can try, but our spells alvays seem to go vrong vhatever ve do,' Valerie said sadly.

'But ve vill try our very very best,' said Wendy.

Valerie and Wendy closed their eyes and began to wave their arms in the air and dance around and around very slowly. As they danced they chanted this magic spell to the magical man whose face you can see in a silvery moon especially at Halloween :

'Iggledee pigiledee, man in the moon,
Pigiledee iggledee, let us out soon,
Magically moonman, use your magic once more,
Moonman magically, please open the door!'

At first nothing whatsoever happened but then, very, very slowly, the door of their dungeon inside the hill began to open. Grrrrroooooaaaaannnnnn.

'It verked, it verked,' Valerie and Wendy cried with delight. 'Our magic spell has verked!'

'It was because your spell didn't have any Wees or Voubleyous in it. I think that's why your spells never work properly, it's because you always get your Wees mixed up with your Voubleyous,' said the Sasha cat.

'Well we don't have time to talk about that now,' the Ben cat shouted, 'we have to stop the children from putting that last block of stone into place at the top of the castle!'

The Ben and Sasha cats ran out of the dungeon with their tails pointing straight up to the sky. At the top of the castle they could see that some of the children were about to lift the last block of stone into place. They ran to the castle walls and, because they were mostly cats, they were able to jump, climb and run up the walls and up/ to the very top of the tower in no time at all.

'Stop, stop,' they shouted to the children, 'you must not put that block into its place!'

'YOU MUST DO AS I SAY,' boomed the Wizard, 'DO NOT LISTEN TO THEM. THEY ARE JUST TWO SILLY CATS. REMEMBER WHEN THE LAST BLOCK IS PUT IN PLACE YOU WILL ALL BE ABLE TO GO HOME TO YOUR FAMILIES AND FRIENDS. SO MY GOOD CHILDREN, PUT THE BLOCK INTO ITS PLACE, NOW!'

The children looked at the Sasha and Ben cats and said, 'We must obey the Wizard. If we obey the Wizard he will set us free and we can go home to our families and friends again.'

The Sasha and Ben cats jumped to where the last block was to be placed but the children pushed them out of the way. 'Go away cats, we have to do what our master the Wizard has told us to do.'

The children pushed the block closer and closer to where it was to go. 'One more push and we will have done it,' the children cheered. 'One more push and we will be free. Ready now, all together, Puuusssssssshhhhhhhhhh.'

The Sasha and Ben cats watched helplessly as children put their shoulders to the last stone for one last push. Then, just as it seemed that all was lost, they heard a whooshing sound. They looked and saw that it was Scary Bones, in his scariest bright silver, whooshing up towards the castle on the Red String!

Scary Bones whooshed around the children who were pushing the block and made the most frightening sounds that he could make.

'*OoooOOooooOOoooooo, OOOoooOOOooooo OOOOOooooooooooo*'.

The sudden arrival of Scary Bones, flying in the scariest way that he could, frightened the children so much that they let go of the stone block. The stone block fell from the tower, crashed to the ground and then bounced away down to the bottom of the castle's steep hill.

When the children saw the block of stone fall to the bottom of the hill, they became very angry. 'Now we have got to start all over again,' they shouted, 'and it's all because of you!' And they pointed angrily at Scary Bones and the Sasha and Ben cats. They were so very angry that they were not afraid of Scary Bones or anything anymore.

'Get out of our way,' they cried and pushed Scary Bones and the Sasha and Ben cats out of their way. 'We are going to get that block and put it in its place at the top of the castle!'

The children began to march like an angry army of ants down the hill towards the block.

'Skeletons, skeletons,' Scary Bones shouted. 'Stop the children, stop the children. They must not be allowed to put that last block of stone in place!'

The skeletons all flew to the block and stood in front of it like an army of bony soldiers to stop the children from getting to it.

'BE BRAVE MY CHILDREN,' the Wizard boomed. 'THEY ARE ONLY SKELETONS. THEY ARE NOTHING BUT BONES. YOU CAN DEFEAT THEM AND WIN YOUR FREEDOM!'

The children marched on towards the skeletons. The skeletons remained standing in front of the stone block and it looked as if there was going to be the biggest of big battles between the skeletons and the children. The children got closer and closer to the skeletons. A big battle was just about to begin when Valerie and Wendy ran into the last bit of space between the children and the skeletons. Valerie held up her lollipop which said 'STOP CHILDREN' in front of the children and Wendy held hers up in front of the skeletons. Of course, both the children and the skeletons had to stop or they would have been breaking the law.

'Vait children, hear vhat ve have to shout,' Wendy shouted.

'Yes,' shouted Valerie, 'hear vhat ve have to shout. There is no need for you to do vhat the Vizard tells you to do anymore. He has locked all of his vicked vitches inside Holly trees. They can't make you vork for him anymore and there is nothing that he can do to you because he is trapped in the castle. You are already free!'

The children looked around and saw what the two lollipop ladies were saying was true. They cheered and cheered and cheered. 'We are free!' they shouted. 'We don't have to work for the Wizard anymore and we can all go home, home to our families and to our friends!'

'LISTEN TO ME, LISTEN TO ME,' boomed the Wizard, 'DO WHAT I SAY OR YOU WILL ALL BE SORRY!'

The children just laughed back at him. 'There's nothing that you can do to us. You are trapped inside the castle and we are free and there's nothing that you can do about it!'

'But there is something that we can do about him,' the Sasha and Ben cats called from the top of the tower. 'If we make the castle a ruin again then the Wizard will never ever be able to escape from it to rule the world again!'

The children cheered. 'Yes, that's what we will do.' They ran back up the hill and onto the castle walls. They began throwing off the blocks that the witches had made them put into the castle. As the children threw them off the blocks bounced down to the bottom of the hill.

'STOP AT ONCE,' the Wizard boomed, 'I COMMAND YOU TO STOP AT ONCE!'

The children took no notice of him and kept throwing the blocks off the castle.

'STOP I TELL YOU,' the Wizard boomed less boomingly than before, 'I COMMAND YOU TO STOP AT ONCE!'

The children kept throwing the blocks off which then bounced down to the bottom of the hill.

'STOP I TELL YOU!' As the children threw off more and more blocks to bounce down the hill, the Wizard boomed even less boomingly than before.

'I COMMAND YOU TO STOP AT ONCE!'

The children took no notice of him.

'STOP, STOP, PLEASE STOP,' the Wizard was booming very quietly now and soon his boom faded away completely. 'PLEASE STOP, I PROMISE THAT I WON'T EVER DO ANYTHING......'

The Wizard's booming faded away. He had disappeared back into the ruins where he will stay for ever and ever, and perhaps even longer than that.

'Hoorah, hoorah,' the children and the skeletons cheered. 'Now let's all go home to Wareham!'

With Valerie and Wendy and their lollipops right in front, and with Scary Bones and the Sasha and Ben cats right behind them, and then all of the children and all the of skeletons behind them, they all set off towards Wareham town and home.

As they reached the town bridge the skeletons realised that it was nearly morning and remembered that they had to be back in the graveyard before the sun rose again in the east.

'We will have to go,' they said and flew off towards the graveyard waving and calling, 'Goodbye everybody' as they went. Scary Bones, all of the children and Valerie and Wendy waved and called out to the skeletons as they flew off, 'thank you, skeletons, thank you for saving us all, we will never forget you. Goodbyeeeeeee!'

'It's time for us to go home too,' the children said. 'Thank you for saving us Mr Scary Bones, and thank you strange-looking cats, and thank you lollipop ladies.' And, still saying their '*goodbyes*' as they left, the children went off to their families and homes.

The only ones left standing on the bridge now were Scary Bones, the two cats which were Sasha and Ben, and Valerie and Wendy.

'What is going to happen to us?' asked Sasha and Ben. 'Are we going to be cats for ever now?'

'No, no,' Valerie and Wendy said. 'Ve can't let that happen, can ve? Ve vill have to rewerse our spell, now how did it go?'

At that very moment the great bell of Wareham Church began to ring out. Dooonnngggggggg.......

'Yes, that's it,' they cried and they began to wave their arms and dance and chant round the Sasha and Ben cats to reverse their magic spell,

> '*Ding dong bell,*
> *Release these children from the spell*
> *That turned them into cats*
> *And give us back our proper... HATS.*'

In less time than it takes to go from here to there, or even from there to here, there was a claaaaaaap of thunder, a ꟻLASH of lightening and four puffs of smoke.

When two of the puffs of smoke had blown away with the wind, Sasha and Ben were standing there exactly as they had been before they had been turned into cats.

When the other two puffs of smoke blew away, Valerie and Wendy were standing there but they didn't look like witches any more, they looked like any other happy and friendly lollipop ladies. They were both wearing lollipop lady yellow coats and little lollipop lady hats with peaks. Their eyes were a sparkling blue instead of bright green, and even Valerie's long droopy nose was dry and hairless.

'Well, well,' the ladies said, 'we all seem to be back to normal again.'

'What did you say?' asked Scary Bones, Sasha and Ben in complete surprise.

'We said that we all seem to be back to normal again,' the ladies said.

'But can't you hear?' Sasha and Ben said. 'You have stopped getting your Wees mixed up with your Vubbleyous.'

'So we have,' said the ladies and they laughed and laughed. But now, when they laughed, they laughed just like two happy lollipop ladies rather than cackling like two wicked witches.

They turned to Scary Bones and held his bony hands. 'We have to go now but before we go we have to thank you for saving us all Mr Scallywag, or can we call you Scary Bones now that we know your proper name?'

Scary Bones laughed and nodded his head so hard that his teeth rattled so loudly that everyone laughed.

'Well, we will see you all in the morning,' said Valerie and Wendy and they walked away into the town taking their lollipops with them.

Scary Bones and the children went back to their Grandma's house and crept in so quietly that she didn't even know that they had been out for most of the night. When they got back to their bedroom Scary Bones stepped into his grey box and the Red String curled up in one of the corners and was soon sleeping as happily as a new born kitten.

'Well that was another exciting adventure you got me into,' said Scary Bones. 'But I must go, I need to get some sleep too you know, and so goodbye until we meet again.' With that Scary Bones turned into a golden glow and disappeared.

'We barely had chance to say 'good bye' to him,' said Ben, 'but we need to get to sleep too.'

As soon as their heads touched their pillows, and perhaps even sooner than that, Ben and Sasha fell fast asleep.

After eating their breakfast the next morning Sasha and Ben went into the town. At the crossroads Valerie and Wendy were stopping the traffic to let the town's children go to school. As the children crossed the road the ladies were giving something to every single one of them. Sasha and Ben were wondering what on earth it could be when the two ladies beckoned to show that they, the two ladies, wanted to speak to them.

When they reached the ladies, the ladies showed Sasha and Ben what they had been giving to the children. They were round orange badges with a drawing of Scary Bones and these words on them :

'I ♥ Scary Bones'

'We have had these badges made for children everywhere so that they will never ever forget how Scary Bones saved us all from the wicked Wizard of Corfe Castle,' Valerie said.

'So here is a badge for you, Sasha. Here is one for you, Ben. And here is one for Scary Bones,' Wendy said.

'And these,' Valerie said, 'are for all those other children who would like to be friends of Scary Bones,' and she handed them a bag full of the orange badges.

'Please make sure that Scary Bones gets his badge,' Valerie said, 'so that he will remember us all. And then please give the other badges to those children who like Scary Bones as much as we do. Will you do that for us?'

'Yes of course we will, or at least we will try our very hardest to do it,' the children said.

When they arrived back at their Grandma's house they went straight to their bedroom. They dropped the badge for Scary Bones into his grey box and, as it touched the bottom of the box, there was a puff of smoke and it disappeared. Then they put the other badges into envelopes and dropped those into Scary Bones' box too. As each one touched the bottom of the box, it disappeared in a puff of smoke just like Scary

Bones' badge had. And do you know that from that day to this, not one of those envelopes with a Scary Bones' badge inside it has ever been seen again?

But, after reading our story, you do know some important things. You know now why no-one has ever tried to rebuild Corfe Castle again because, if anyone ever did, then the powerful wicked Wizard would escape from it and rule the world again. You know why some holly trees have spikey prickly leaves and why, as Halloween approaches, their green berries begin to turn to bright red. And you know why those berries are poisonous to eat.

But do you know this? That from that day to this, a proper wicked witch has never ever been seen in the little town of Wareham again, ...

or so some people say!

The End.

The Bridge at Wareham Town

The author would like to record his sincere thanks to the pupils and teachers of Anderton Park School, Milldown School, and Sandroyd School, Bookbabblers, Huckleberry Books and to all those friends, parents, teachers and other children who contributed in so many ways to the publication of this story.

This is the fourth in 'The Amazing Adventures of Scary Bones the Skeleton' series. The other stories are :

The Lost Dog and Bone : This first adventure tells how Sasha and Ben meet Scary Bones and the Red String for the very first time. The town dogs have all disappeared and Scary Bones has lost a bone. In the adventure that follows they meet the terrible dog-nappers Snatchet and Grabbet, and Mrs. Grumble.

The Pirates of Brownsea Island : Scary Bones, Sasha and Ben are captured by pirates who are after old Captain Grow Bag's treasure which is buried on Brownsea Island. Helped by the island's Red Squirrels, our heroes save it for us all to enjoy for ever.

The Dinosaurs of the Jurassic Coast : Scary Bones, Sasha and Ben are locked in a lost world of monster dinosaurs and cavemen. Helped by Durdle Doorus, the friendliest and happiest of dinosaurs, they escape and the famous Durdle Door is created.

The Nasty Romans of Maiden Castle : Our heroes are whisked back to Roman Britain by the Celtic Queen Do-you-see-her. They are captured by nasty Romans and made to fight two fierce gladiators and a lion in the arena. Can they escape and get back home again?

Every Scary Bones adventure has a mysterious sealed envelope that should not be opened until the end of the story.

MTBooks
Mulberry Tree Books
Mulberry House
Winterborne Stickland
Dorset DT11 0NT
www.mulberrytreebooks.co.uk